SWEET DREAMS STORIES

A collection of bedtime tales

p

This book
belongs to…

● ● ● ● ● ● ● ● ● ●

● ● ● ● ● ● ● ● ●

CONTENTS

On my
own
5

If you hold
my
hand
33

Just

as well, really!
61

This is a Parragon Book
This edition published in 2002
Parragon, Queen Street House,
4 Queen Street, Bath BA1 1HE, UK

Created and produced by
The Complete Works

ISBN 0-75259-048-0

Printed in China

On my
own

Written by Jillian Harker
Illustrated by Louise Gardner

Deep in the jungle, where only wild things go, Mungo's mum was teaching him what a young monkey needs to know.

"Some things just aren't safe to try alone," she said.

"Why not?" said Mungo crossly. "I'm big enough to do things–

on my own!"

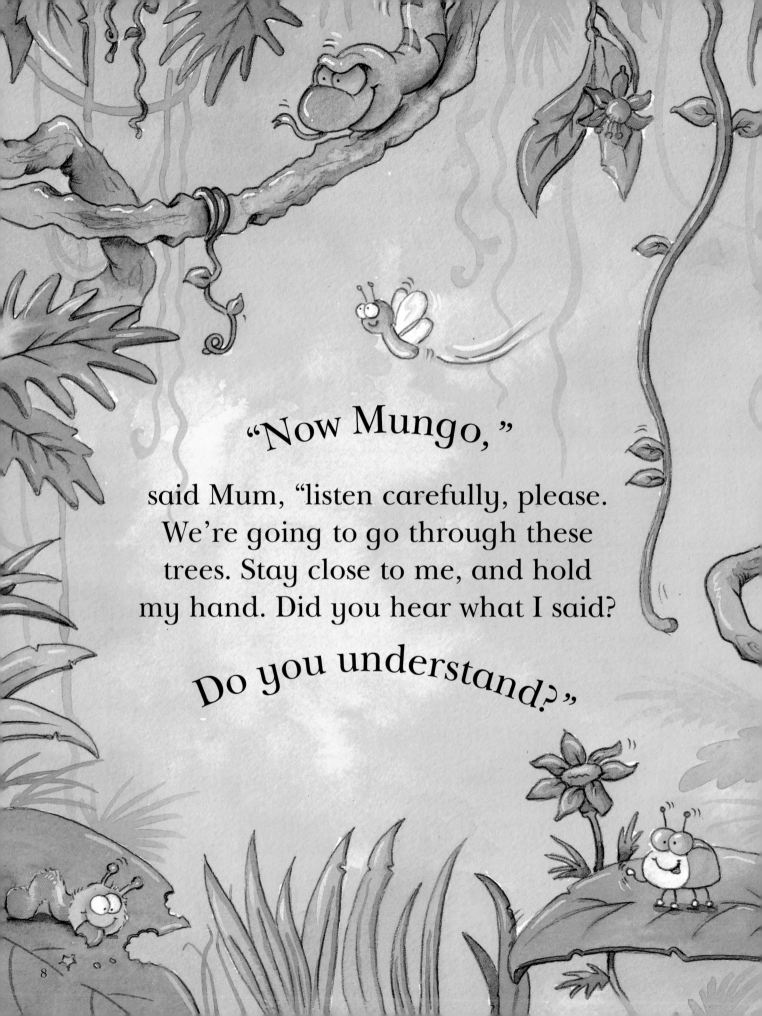

"Now Mungo,"

said Mum, "listen carefully, please. We're going to go through these trees. Stay close to me, and hold my hand. Did you hear what I said?

Do you understand?"

"It's okay, Mum. I won't slip or fall. I can swing across there with no trouble at all," said Mungo. "I'm big enough to do it—
on my own!" And off he swung!

"Hissss," hissed Snake, in a snake sort of wail.

"That pesky Mungo pulled my tail!"

And did Mungo hear poor old Snake groan?

No!
Mungo just laughed.
"I told you I could do it
on my own."

"Now, we're going to cross the river using these stones," said Mum. "But, Mungo, I'd rather you didn't do this alone."

"But Mum," said Mungo, and he ran on without stopping, "I'm really good at jumping and hopping. I'm big enough to do it –

on my own!"

And off he sprang!

"That Mungo trampled on my nose!" said Croc.

"Next time, I'll nibble off his toes!"

And did Mungo hear poor old Croc groan?

No! Mungo just smiled. "I told you I could do it on my own."

"Mungo," said Mum, with a serious look on her face, "the jungle can be a dangerous place. There are all sorts of corners for creatures to hide, so, from here on, make sure that you stay by my side."

"Oh, Mum," said Mungo, "I don't need to wait for you. I can easily find my own way through. I'm big enough to do it—

on my own!"

Lion rubbed the lump on his nose.

"O_uch!

That Mungo's so careless!" he said.

And did Mungo hear poor old Lion groan?
No! Mungo just grinned. "I told you I could do it
on my own."

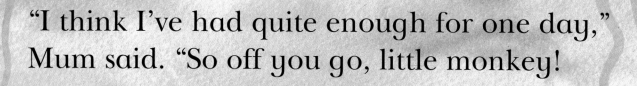

"I think I've had quite enough for one day," Mum said. "So off you go, little monkey!

Now it really is time for bed!"

It was Mungo's turn to let out a groan.

"I don't want to go to bed –
on my own!"

"Don't worry," said Mum. "Come on,
kiss me goodnight, and I promise I'll
hold you and cuddle you tight."

Lion roared, "Is that Mungo still awake?" "Yes!" snapped Crocodile.

"Let's help him go to sleep," hissed Snake.

And into the velvety, starry sky drifted
the sounds of a jungle lullaby.

31

If you hold my hand

Written by Jillian Harker

Illustrated by Andy Everitt-Stewart

Oakey's mum opened the front door. "Come on, Oakey. Let's go outside and explore."

ROSE COTTAGE

But Oakey wasn't really sure. He was only small, and the world looked **big** and scary.

"*Only if you promise to hold my hand,*" said Oakey.

So Oakey's mum led him down the long lane. Oakey wished he was back at home again!

"This looks like a great place to play. Shall we take a look? What do you say?" asked Oakey's mum.

"*Only if you hold my hand,*" said Oakey.

And Oakey did it!

"Look at me! I can do it!" he cried.

"This slide looks fun. Would you like to try?" asked Oakey's mum.

Oakey looked at the ladder. It **stretched** right up to the sky.

"I'm only small," said Oakey. "I don't know if I can climb that high—
unless you hold my hand."

And Oakey did it!

"Wheee! Did you see me?" he cried.

"We'll take a short cut through the wood," said Oakey's mum.

"I'm not sure if we should," said Oakey. "It looks dark in there. Well, I suppose we could—will you hold my hand?"

And Oakey did it!

"Boo! I scared you!" he cried.

Deep in the wood, Oakey found a stream, shaded by beautiful tall trees.

"Stepping stones, look!"
said Oakey's mum.
"Do you think you could jump
across these?"

"Maybe," said
Oakey. "I just need you
to hold my hand, please."

And Oakey did it!

One…

two…

three...

four...

"Your turn now, Mum," cried Oakey,
holding out his hand.

Beyond the wood, Oakey and his mum ran up the hill, and all the way down to the sea.

"Come on, Oakey," called his mum.

54

"Would you like to paddle in the sea with me?"

But the sea looked **big**, and he was only small.

Suddenly, Oakey
knew that didn't
matter at all.
He turned to
his mum and

smiled...

"I can do anything if you hold my hand," he said.

the end

Just
as well, really!

Written by Jillian Harker
Illustrated by Julie Nicholson

Rumpus liked water.

He liked the drippiness and droppiness,

the splashiness and sloppiness of it!

He liked it so much that, whenever there was water around…

But Mum loved Rumpus, so

every time, she simply sighed—and she mopped up the mess.

Rumpus loved
mud.

He loved the way
you could
plodge
in it,

splodge

in it,

slide
in it and
glide

in it!

He loved it so much that, whenever
there was mud around...

But Dad loved Rumpus, so

every time, he simply sighed – and
he sponged off the splatters.

Rumpus enjoyed paint.

He liked to
splatter
and
dash it,

to spread
and
splash
it!

74

He enjoyed it so much that,
whenever there was paint around…

But Rumpus' brother loved him, so

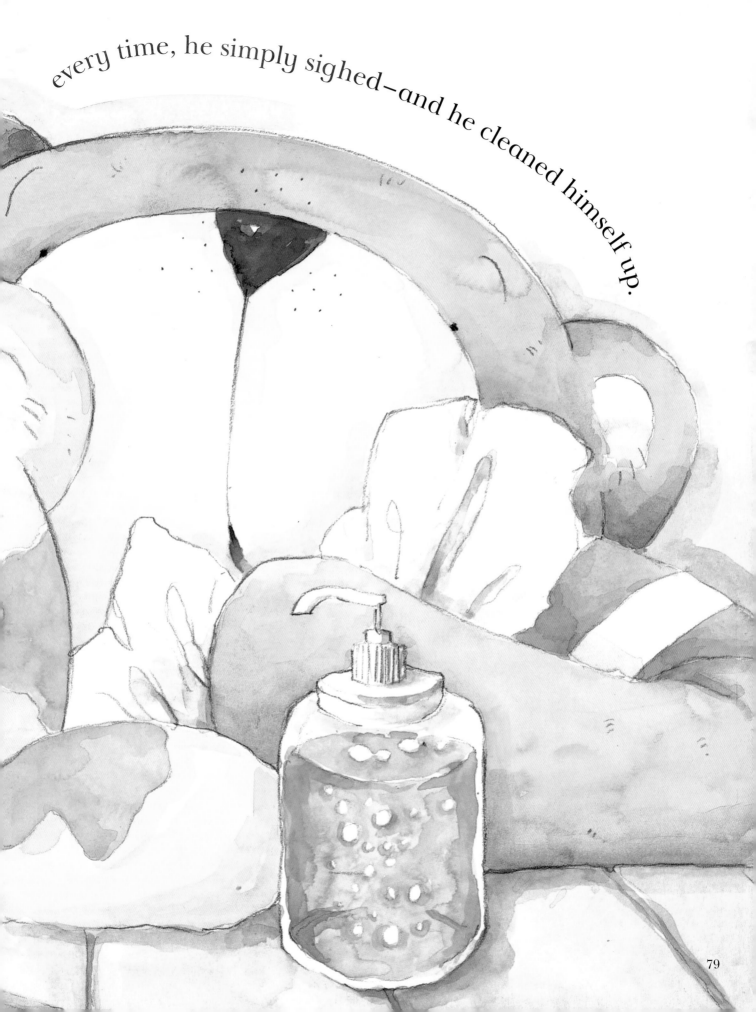

every time, he simply sighed—and he cleaned himself up.

Rumpus liked to find out how things worked.

He loved the prodding and probing,

the **wiggling** and the **jiggling**, the unscrewing and the undoing!

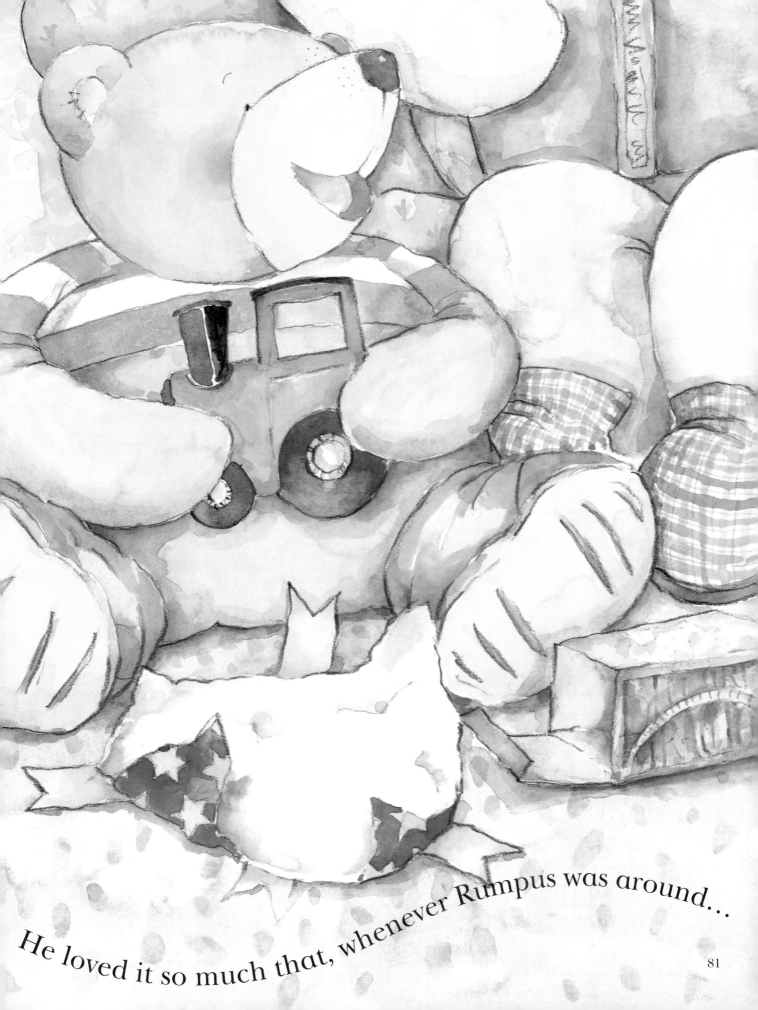

He loved it so much that, whenever Rumpus was around...

...things didn't work for long!

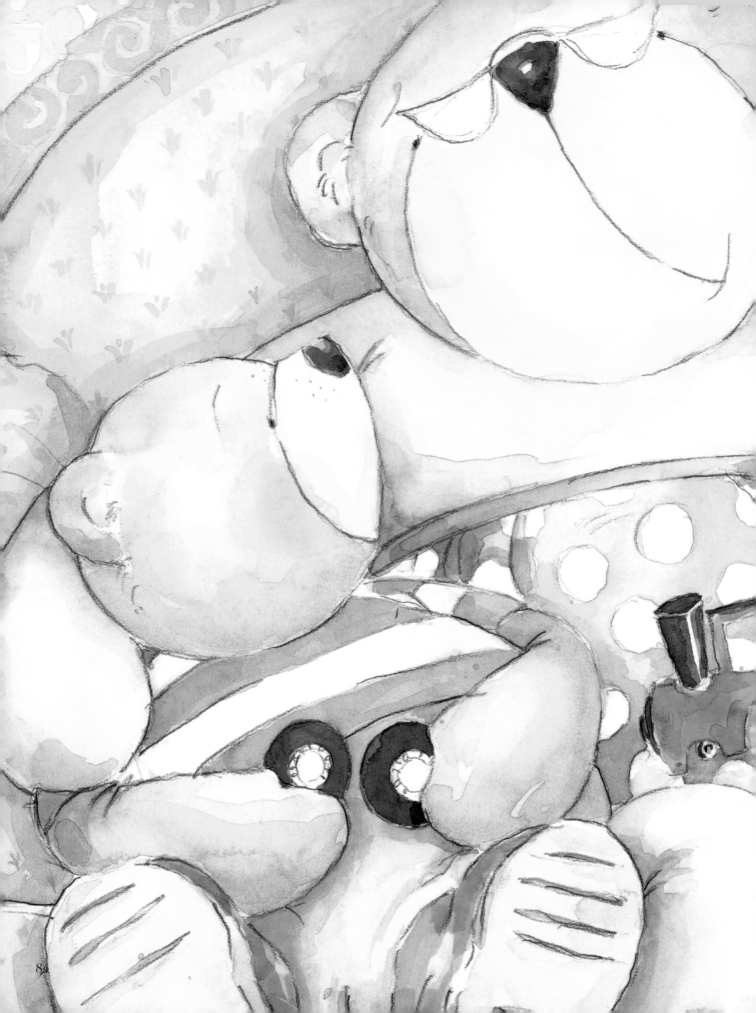

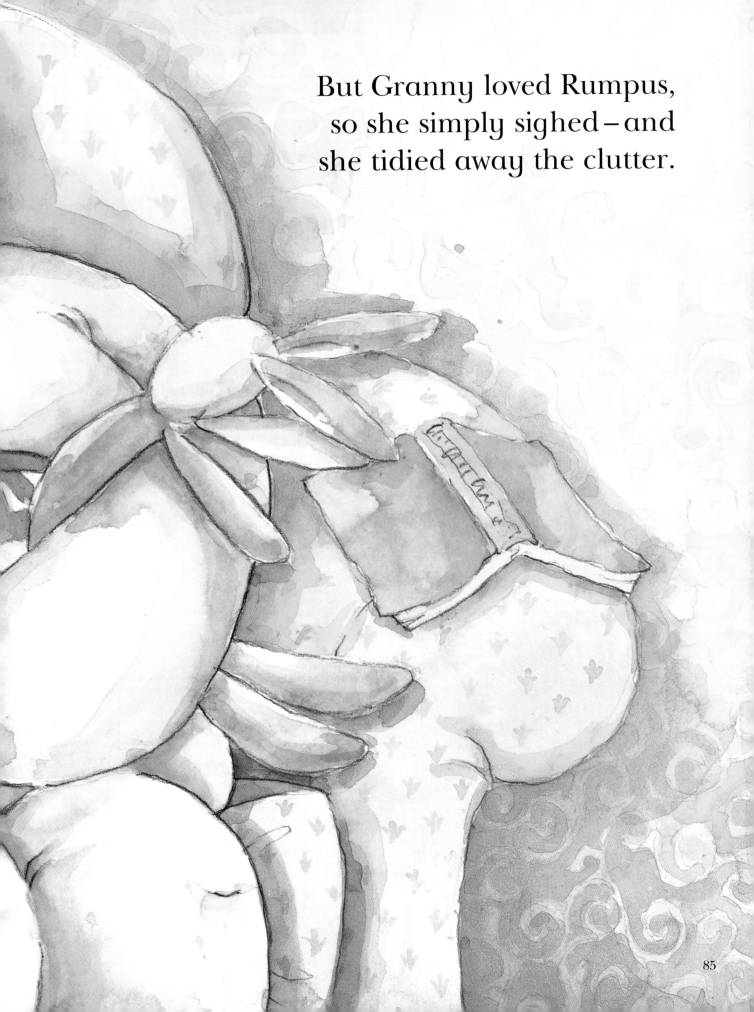

But Granny loved Rumpus,
so she simply sighed—and
she tidied away the clutter.

Rumpus loved his mum, dad…

brother and granny…

Rumpus' mum, dad, brother and granny loved Rumpus…

…just as well, really!

the end